dreamboat

To Peter & Hazel —

With love —

[signature]

Also by d.k. jones

Stickman

Mixed Blessings

dreamboat

SKETCHES

d.k. jones

Ginabean books

The author gratefully acknowledges the encouragement of Tracy Jones and Carey Jones Danen with special thanks to Stuart McCarty for his invariably patient guidance.

Library of Congress Catalog Card Number 98-94152

ISBN 0-9640186-2-4

Cover design by Stuart McCarty

Cover illustration by Brian Van Keulen and Tara Wilson

Printed at The Geryon Press
Tunnel, New York

For Jess and Brett

I scarcely know where to begin,
but love is always a safe place.

EMILY DICKINSON

No human being can really understand
another, and no one can arrange
another's happiness.

GRAHAM GREENE

CONTENTS

dreamboat

IMMORTAL

The hammered coppery pot or vase is from a Beirut flea market. He got it in Sixty-two. The pot didn't mean that much to him but the girl who spent nearly an hour making sure he got a "fair" price did. Like a lot of people there she had two first names, a christian name and an arabic name. She used one or the other depending on which part of the city she was in. A year later she died of a brain tumor. Just before her twenty-ninth birthday. Her kindness never left him. There were a lot of dead people in his life. Said he lived among the dead.

See that black and white painting of a sailing ship on plastered ceramic. It was done 'specially for him in Savona on the Ligurian seacoast in Italy. He'd get sick on baby octopus he didn't think he could refuse from his Italian host and then walk over to see how the work was coming. He stayed on there for days because the artisan hadn't finished it yet. Those blue tiles are from a village in Brazil.

She got them in Sixty-nine. They were going to have them inlaid as a table top, then discovered they didn't have enough. He was going to get some more but he never got to it. Life is like that you know.

Now the handsome hand carved horse with precious looking stones and chain reins is from Puebla, Mexico. One of a kind. That beauty was a favorite of a lot of folks. When it was brought here by a friend, it was buckled into its own seat on an airplane. It had to be unwrapped enroute because the captain and the crew wanted to see it.

Did he get something from everywhere?

No. He wasn't a collector. Just what was given him or what he brought as gifts. Each one of these things was a link to the people along his way. There was always a story behind each piece or it came from a place he cared about.

When he got old why didn't he get rid of them. He got rid of most stuff.

Said he was going to get rid of all that stuff. Reminded him too much of when they were immortal.

Did he — get rid of it?

No. I knew he wouldn't. Just be a sign he was giving up.
He was very chic once. Enjoyed fine things. Always said he
didn't give a rat's ass, but a part of him did. People are like
that you know.

FROGTOWN GIRL

I went to her church expressly for the purpose of viewing her. So did Slade on a different Sunday. One row behind, across the aisle to the left so she might not know I was watching her steadily. I got some real looks from the people around me. When she came out she walked with her hands stuffed in her warmup jacket pockets. Something about that made her more beautiful than ever. She grinned at me big time like she knew I'd been watching her the whole time.

After that I started going over to her house in Frogtown. We couldn't go places because we didn't have money. First we'd sit on the front steps smoking her mother's Lucky Strikes. Then go in the house and neck. She tasted so good. In daylight we watched the freight cars pulled back and forth in the switchyard across the road. Once in awhile a brakeman waved at us. After dark we'd listen to freight cars being switched, banging into each other and then watch the Northern Lights. Inside the house life was more down at the heel than I was used to. One threadbare sofa we filled end to end, if we could, when her little brother wasn't on it. She had two sweaters, one on and one in the wash. Sunday shoes and her other shoes. She could care less and high school proms were not on her horizon.

It was the same drill with Slade. We sort of took turns over there and reported the same experience. We were interchangeable. We knew she was the best kisser in the whole town, wet or moist in all the right places and she worshiped us. Heaven on earth.

My live in maiden aunt didn't think so. "Why must you go way over there where those hunyaks live and date a Lutheran girl when you know it sorrows your mother and father so. There are plenty of Catholic girls right here in the neighborhood," she said, as if plenty, Catholic and neighborhood made for me what they made for her; a divine trinity. A beer every other Saturday at a local tavern with a spinster friend was her brush with sin.

Eventually we got worn down.
"There's no future in this," Slade said one day.
"Why not?"
"She's an outsider."
"So what?"
"We're not, that's what. We got a chance to go to college, maybe law school, get rich, pillars of the community, all

that. She's got a chance to be a diner waitress all her life. You couldn't get through a hotel lobby with her."

"You outa' your mind, Slade, she's only sixteen years old!"

"I'm tellin' ya," he insisted.

Yet Slade was the one she rode off with one day. Had straddled him and pinned his shoulders to the flatbed of a Chevy pickup while the driver sped off so quick you wondered where the fire was. I never saw her again.

Slade called from Vegas a few months later where he was trying to get a job dealing blackjack. Said there was jobs come on out. Last time he saw her she was in Phoenix holdin' on to some guy with both hands.

We never could demystify her.

Awhile back I saw in the newspaper that her mother, at last elderly, had died. We couldn't imagine her mother elderly, just frozen in her thirties. She herself, named in the obituary, was living in California. Well that's what the paper said. To Slade and me she still lived in some corner of us.

"That was the beauty of knowing people," Slade had said, "You always kept something of who they were."

LOVE CHILD

(In a bizarro screen treatment)

EXTERIOR. OLD MAN ON PARK BENCH. Sticky sweet fifties music through title and opening narration. VOICE-OVER OF OLD MAN.

The following for the record, in the light
Of everything before and since;
One bright summer afternoon, nineteen-fifty
Something, Eisenhower still the Boss,
Organized religion, outward servant of the bossed
Proclaims The Devil is influencing music. Again.
Woe be to the self indulgent and
Unmarried pregnant women.
Rowdy, the guilty party, troubled, seeks advice
From a college professor and French priest.
Only one he knows who is not Righteous.
Cut. Print. Next set up.

7

Rowdy and his girl have made a baby
In a Ford or Chevy
The All-American way.
French priest listens knowledgeably, he is French
After all.
But he goes astray in home truths out of
Mathew Arnold, Yeats, Auden, Eliot.
Rowdy brings him back.

*Medium shot entering weedy ghost town with closeup to road
sign that says — WELCOME TO HELL — POP — the rest
of the word worn away or unfinished.*

Cut back to priest's quarters

She weel go to New York to have thees babee?
Yes.
No abortion.
Absolutely not.
She ees strong to do thees thing alone, no?
Stubborn.
Geeve hair credeet my friend. She does what
She theenks she must do. To have your visit,
Would make it hardair.

8

A harmonica is heard playing "New York, New York" but
becomes lost under a tuba booming: "Sioux City Sue."

Camera for no apparent reason
Pans to cow in meadow.
Point of view, Rowdy. Mad as hell. And sad.
Wishing nineteen-sixty-nine. Or ninety-nine.
No such thing as world-wide gawk.
No missed trueness.
Keep baby. Avoid fraudulent trauma. Misplaced
Anguish.
Testosterone no longer an illegal drug.
No long life holding a deception.
Or words to that effect.
Dissolve.
Producer wants to cut this scene,
Keep fifties blithering artifice.
Director livid, wants to quit.

Incurably lonely
Rowdy and girl need to talk.
But choose sexual overload.
Their real life is the bed.
After she flew away, he walked head down,
Seeing her in birthing stirrups.
Has a job and always late. Liquid lunches.
Meets pretty girl; face lights up, at once
Goes into shock as though an unseen
Fire hose has turned on him.

Frees a moth but
Craves rough, authentic human contact.
Anything that is not gratuitous violence.

*Cut to phone ringing on hallway table. Low, deep double bass
in background. Rowdy picks it up.*

You o.k.?
Yes.
The baby?
Yes. A handsome boy.
Did you have a lot of difficulty?
No.
How are you now?
I'm fine.
When do you give him up?
Day after tomorrow…
…When will you be back?…

What's wrong?, Rowdy's mother asks as he hangs up.
Nothing, he says, trying to clear his throat.
She's coming back in a couple of weeks.
He walks by her, going out back door,
His breathing ragged, chest tight.
Won't come back in until they are all sleeping.

That voice again.

The following for the record, in the light
Of everything before and since;
A year later, Rowdy married her.
They lived with their secret,
Happily ever after.

*Ghost town again. Cold winter. Nativity scene where the road
sign was. Except the crib is empty. All statuary figures look
frightened to see their own breath. Frame begins long dissolve to
the sound of Neil Diamond's "Hello My Friend, Hello." Bring
up credits.*
Screen goes to dark.

> *I only know that what is moral is what
> you feel good after and what is immoral
> is what you feel bad after.*
>
> Ernest Hemingway

FIRST LIGHT

I wondered who would see you and date you next, grasping
for the danger of your hand. And if they would drown you
in flattery. Then all of them speechless, overcome by your
Chantilly. I am certain in my sleep, I will lose you.
Something will take me away. The Army. A poison a rival
has hid in my food. I dreamt your voice on the phone, a
cold gruff tone I never heard before. *You must give it up now*
— hanging up, me hanging there almost seeing you turn
my picture to the wall.

*

The full drink in front of me roils with you, but when it is
drained I have drunk your storm and like God, I almost
doubt if you exist. Out on the sunny street I discover one
drink is not enough — from you there is no shelter. If you
ask me to return your little snapshot — I shall say I lost it
and you will know at once it is a lie.

*

I remind myself how young you are. Perhaps you are not ready for this — Do you really know what you are doing. I have been ready since my kindergarten spring. Promises. No. Promises are fool's gold. I promise only I will not bore you.

*

My body makes a prayer while walking to the college not knowing it has done so. I have forgotten my books, my classes. The street I am walking on has forgotten its name.

*

I get up in the dark and smoke. Bugs bang the screen wanting the glow of the weed. Are you awake or sleeping easy. Am I the letter lost between the pages of your book — and you the next Bride of Christ.

*

I am helping to make the Shepard Road. Asphalt raker. Flagman. Huber roller driver. Shoveler. One and all those sometime that day. We are behind schedule and work through lunch. Prisoners taking only water. Heat, dirt, jackhammers; sweating shirtless men slightly woozy from all the fumes. One of them nudges me and says to look up there where you are waving. Standing at the top of the fire escape where you work, obviously beautiful even from that distance. The crew, now all eyes and genitals, learn the meaning of liberation. If you do not care, why have you come out as Juliet on that frail balcony.

*

Must I get up at first light to be the first one to take you in my arms. Whoever matters most will be first in the morning and last at night.

DREAMBOAT

I am pretty sick. Nearly dead I'm told later. Unconscious in the base hospital with a sky high fever and the doctors can't figure it out. Then some French army doctor on an exchange program gives me a spinal. He thinks it's either polio or neural meningitis. Eventually I come around but can't move my arms much and don't know what's going on most of the time.

Then one day I'm half asleep and I get a whiff of this dreamboat from home coming through the door. She hasn't even reached the bed yet and I think I'm going to live. She touches me and my body comes alive and I know I'm going to make it. I can't do much with her in these circumstances; she just visits for a few days and when they decide I'm out of the woods she goes back home. I can just imagine the effect she had on the males on the Post, them wondering what planet she fell out of.

They say I can go home for thirty days on a convalescent leave and then come back and almost start over again. I tell them I'm too ill to be of any use to them but they don't buy. I tell them the country must be in bad shape if it really needs a PFC who can't lift a rifle. They don't see any humor in that. First they have to watch me awhile. I am not mending very fast and have lost beaucoup weight. One day an orderly comes in with a projector and a portable screen and they run "Three-Ten To Yuma" with Glenn Ford. The next day they haul it over to another ward and I go there and see it. I even learn some of the lines. Through this wait I imagine her all the time, observing her marvelously slow movement, helpless. I might be willing to die if I can have one more week with her. This is not a good looking, rowdy siren goddess on ten inch heels. This is more an earthmother, the poem of her a manslayer. I laze the days. If a part of me does not heal up, so be it, so long as it is not impotence. I think of Hemingway's Jake Barnes and Lady Brett and all that dreariness. I need more education. Not from books exactly but more a view of existence. How to have each other in a time of leisure, in food and conversation. She would be comfortable in any society. Another letter comes. *Dearest, I needed to write again…*Nothing is like that moment. I remember when we first met. I had come into the house to pick her up. Cold November evening. Someone in her family went to tell her I was there. When she came out smiling broadly, I didn't know which part of her to look at first. It was too much to take in all at once. Sort of like an exotic gift you put away until you have time to enjoy it by yourself. When I helped

16

her into a black velvet coat with a hood I nearly fainted. I hoped she couldn't hear me breathing.

Finally they send me on leave. My uniform doesn't fit and I have trouble lifting my duffel bag onto the train, everybody looking at me like I'm a poor excuse for a soldier in the U.S. Army. I wish I could get into civilian clothes but I don't have any. The countryside flies by. I am embarrassed that the aisles jumping and lurching and dancing to the clack-clack are more difficult to negotiate. I had grown up on trains. We run through Missouri almost due north headed for Kansas City. There are more Redcaps in and out of Neosho than there are in bigger Joplin. At Harrisonville we sit for a long time for no apparent reason. I should be used to that but this time I wish I was on an airplane. We still have a full state and part of two more to go.

I love watching people on trains. After they've settled in they drift into their naturalness. They get comfortable with the motion and read or play or sleep. They open themselves up. When they look out the window I can almost enter their lives. Where they were raised, if they really want to go where they are going. But if they think I am watching them they change. What they were dissolves. They have been compromised.

After awhile a large boned woman dressed in yellow, a little girl about seven lagging her, asks if I'd mind if they sit across from me. Once in, the mother sighs, relieved to be out of the churning aisle. Her face looks like it has seen a lot of road and long nights. She thinks it might be polite to start a conversation but doubts she wants to, arranging her daughter and her things and wiping the window on her side with her sweater sleeve. She checks a tattoo on one ankle and a bracelet on the other. Has called attention to them because she suspects they are her best feature and she's right. The little treasure across from me announces she is Amy and she loves horses and Brian and, nearly breathless, is going to visit someone who is sick. Who is sick she does not say and I do not ask. "What's your name?", she asks almost apologetically. I make one up that sounds like a movie star and tell her, not wanting, just then, to be me. "Do you like being a soldier?" "It's O.K.," I lie again. Her mother tells her not to pester me. "I'm not," she objects, offended. Soon she gets into a coloring book, at first unhappily obedient then rapt, no soldier in her life.

Still an hour out and I'm standing between coaches smoking in the rush of air, listening to the metal groaning and the couplers threatening to disconnect. Gave up sitting when we crossed the state line. Getting stronger by the minute. When the Conductor comes rolling through, he needs to holler to be heard. "You look a lot better now than you did this morning, soldier," smiling. "Yes Sir, thank you." I would have given him my name. My real name. At the station we just crawl in and I look for her long before it's even possible. Then when I almost turn away, there is dreamboat, standing on the platform, dressed to the nines.

As I start to climb down the steps, duffel dragging behind me, I don't hear the trainman say, "watch your step." I am in a hurry. I know exactly how many layers of clothing she has on. And thinking on that I tumble out of the train, ass over teakettle.

FRANCE

The bus driver is looking through his rear view mirror, not at the road just traveled, but at you in a summer cotton. In the vibration of the coach a spaghetti strap slips off your shoulder. If he does not look ahead soon we will crash. We may anyway. He drives back and forth, as if the road is his alone. I seem to be the only worried passenger. I think I will present you to him at lunch. Take the curiosity out of his eyes — pray that he finds some fault — so that in the sleepy afternoon, his mind and body eased, he will concentrate on getting us safely to Cap d'Antibes.

We reach Fontaine for midday picnic. Shaded by gnarly trees, tables wait for us dressed in checkered cloth. Everything happens in slow motion. In a languid breeze we have been given over to indolence. Potage with some legume. Potato and sausage off a chafing dish. Cheese and fruit. Washed down with a cold, dry rouge. I smoke an offered Gauloise and nearly choke. Afterward we linger as if we have nowhere to go. Then all at once we line up and move. A gradual climb to the hills. Hayfields. A church with a weathervane. A small stream with a rowboat tied to a tree. Farms built of stone. As we slow to change direction and lean into a curve, a young boy sits idly on an oxcart watching us pass. He looks like a model for a postcard from any provence, too short shorts above tiny anklets peeking above his shoes, legs perfectly still, never swinging. I decide he is already a stubborn Gaul. We seem to nap in turns, groggy from lunch and the heating day. Going higher still, everything thinning out. Moving slower, the engine straining. Is she sorry we did not fly to Nice? No. We fly enough. This is fascinating. She is right. Slower is often better. Like most, we think we can repeat this any time we want. Like most, we will not come this way again. Another hour and the bus begins to slide out of the Maritime Alps. We are seized with anticipation. When we were born only foreigners who were very rich came to the Riviera. As we descend to the coast, the sun reflecting off the tinfoil Mediterranean is blinding, the endless stretch of sea proof we have reached the end of earth. Someone mentions the vestiges of Roman encampments in this area. I think instead of Napoleon, wondering if he ever saw from this place. If anyone could look on this and still make war.

After checking into our hotel, more a home with but twelve rooms, we explore it. The ground level is consumed with a delicious odor of rich, encrusted soup. Fish a specialty up and down the coast. In the dining room the hardwood creaks, the finish gone from it. There are scattered, generous divans with small aprés-dinner tables placed before them, flowers on alcove window seats look out to the sea. An ordinary moment which seems brilliant discovery. Upstairs more alcoves in the bedroom, the armoir looks and opens like a seventeenth century relic. The bed is smallish with a nautical coverlet. It will do. They all do. Downstairs again. The owner, an apocalypse on a cane, purple cheeked with hands like wood approaches us laughing, warns us this is a place for lovers. We can, he says jubilantly, race our own go-carts in the park tonight, but to watch out for a Sweden man who likes to smash into everyone. In the tiny vestibule, we hadn't noticed coming in, a handmade sign: Poisson, pain, cafe et cognac, vingt-quatre heureux. Help yourself.

We need to walk. A long day on the bus. Across the road, away from the beach, alley streets rise crookedly into hills. As we go higher the water behind us turns from blue to jade. Details enter us, fractions of the town unfolding. Tourists pass with sunburnt faces. The color of stone darkens in the late afternoon. I can't imagine being here alone without you, at least not now, not today. In another life perhaps... the thought passes into oblivion. The sound of heels on mixed surfaces comes up at us. A Frenchman sleeps on a corner bench, brown coat, brown pants. The browns do not match. A little girl walking ahead of us with her mother keeps turning to look at me. We have trouble taking our eyes from each other. I think of what it would be like to have one of those. What it would be like to be the father of a child. The thought joins the other one in oblivion. We turn and go to our right as if we have an instinct to circle back to where we started. Monsieur Greene's apartment is nearby. We go into a flower shop to look. Girls move back and forth behind counters, chalk white skin showing beneath white smocks. Fussing with stems and wrappers, they look up only when they have to. No song on their lips. No ribbons in their hair. I buy a flower. A little bell rings above the door as we go out. We speak of having an evening at Monte Carlo but there is no pressing need. Then we don't talk for a long time. It is cooling down. At a corner back by the hotel, without warning I reach and pull up your dress. You scream and begin to run away, then come back shaking a finger at me. In the streets there is the smell of bread.

To you who will never be able to read this book

Albert Camus

DARK PASSAGE

There were wonderful things in that life. That they were wonderful were not his doing, they simply existed when he did. And some things not. They existed anytime. What the older or wiser might see as trivial or shabby he saw as fresh, carnal and for the moment important. Every grainy cultural nuance, every aura of dissipation, every grubby restaurant and shop, even the best moment at the worst party deserved to be remembered. Breathtakingly ordinary and he knew it wouldn't last. He and his colleagues left a broad wake. Their interest was in the prodigious — riotous nights followed by long working days — or was it the other way round? Sometimes these blended together unfashionably; wrinkled slept-in suits telltale, a pock of shaving cream from a rushed morning shave hanging stubbornly beneath someone's ear. The inevitable revival that occurred late afternoon when he looked out an office window at the yellow headlights rushing down the road toward the smell of night.

He got on the Rue de Malagnou Geneva bus and rode it in circles refusing to get off. He was meant to transfer and go to the airport and depart. The carnal, the important and the riotous shrunk to dried-up crust. His left hand was the color of burgundy from a death grip held on his passport's burgundy coverlet inside his jacket pocket. He felt like a fingerling again scared to go to school. Everything the bus rolled by; buildings, statues, storefronts, the tableaux of the city was the color of burgundy. Then his window smeared with mud or blood, so that his mind's eye could haunt itself. A burgundy girl got on and sat across from him. He wanted her to hold him while he buried his head in her. If he tried to get off the bus, he wanted her to stand and block his way. Today, for the first time, he was afraid to fly.

Carlos is dead. He kept repeating those three words to himself as if repetition would convince. The news had come in a phone call the night before. He was attracted to people who had known the best and the worst, whose life had been anything but a smooth trip. One of these had been his compadre, Carlos Alvarez, a thirty year old Cuban, who had left Havana just before Castro's triumphant entry. Castro was new, Carlos said, but he was a communist and wouldn't last, Carlos more hopeful than sure. That had also been said of Batista but Batista had lasted the most part of twenty-six years. He had met Carlos when they both joined the company. Smart, quick and savvy, Carlos was to work Latin America and be the point man in the development of business in Cuba. He was thrilled by the opportunity and challenge. They ate and drank together, Carlos educating him in the ways of Cubans and other Latinos. They would go to Havana together some time, they were sure of that, and the learning could continue first hand. From the way they talked about it, there was more prospect of play than work. Carlos had a fiancée, his novia, he called her. He carried a snapshot of her and when he and Carlos got together they had a ritual they went through. The photo would come out of a pocket and the two of them would swoon, groaning and falling into each other's arms. Her name was Alejandra and she was beautiful. Carlos himself was perhaps the most handsome young man he had ever seen and he had a charisma. He and his family had been poor, knowing a deprivation not often found in the States. His life had no achievements other than itself. It declared, in its way, there are things that matter and these things one must do. Life is energy, life is desire and he was all of that. Now it is wrenched out, what's left of him, obedient, passed hand to hand in darkness.

They had cleared the runway at the Lima airport and that was about it. Black, foggy and raining and the mountain at the end of it just waiting to smack them. *El montaña diabolico,* some called it. There were no survivors. Regular flyers knew which airports lay at the base of mountains, the information tucked away in the pits of stomachs. He had landed and taken off from there himself and assumed he had been a near miss. Everybody sometime was a near miss. Up to now he had accepted that. Someone would tell him to get advice, help, but those giving the advice would not have known Carlos. The evil of that fate would be beyond them. No one could advise him. He couldn't dissolve an image of Alejandra with her family in Miami, crying, in despair, pounding her fists on a wall like it was the mountain.

He didn't make the plane he was ticketed for but he made the next one. Four hours before he couldn't imagine flying again. Once settled in his seat, he was at least in familiar surroundings. They will close the door in another minute or so and then begin the slow taxi away. He must do something until they are airborne. Fix his mind on a problem or sequence of events. Consider a step-by-step solution to the problem that put him on this aircraft in the first place. No not that. Something that will hold him. Something worth recalling and counting one by one. He thought of Alejandra again, sorry he had never met her. That brought him to the women he had known in his own life. They had mattered. If he had it real bad or they were a taste of things to come, they were important. The tawdry, the tasteful, the manic and the shy. He is not permitted to remember one or two. He must remember them all.

By the time cruising altitude arrived he was more at home. The stewardess smiled at him every time she walked by, denying him his dull pain. She looked a lot like Bacall. Cool and willowy standing in the aisle up ahead, she made him think of somebody's line from *Dark Passage*. Nobody wants to die. There is no such thing as courage — only fear. That's why humans live so long.

THE TOURIST

I know I shouldn't have married below my station.

What are you talking about?

Winthrop, you never wanted to take me to Europe.

We are here because I saved for years.

Someone had to pay for the house.

Harry Hendrick said at dinner last night he was enjoying
the tour; the museums, the cathedrals, everything.

Harry Hendrick's so old he don't know where he is.

Well at least he talks to his wife.

He's a nit-wit.

What?

Nothing.

At breakfast, Marie said the bus is leaving at nine — so we can reach Grenoble for lunch.

Marie is eating her way through Europe.

You don't seem to mind that Carleton woman flirting her way through Europe. I've seen her winking at you.

Nah — she had something in her eye.

Everyday this week?

O.K. She winks at anyone in pants.

What were you doing with that sneaky Frenchman at the Calais yesterday?

Claude?

Why is he with us, he's from here?

He's lonely.

He's sneaky.

You think all French are sneaky.

They are. Why were you so long there?

It's a quiet outdoor cafe — away from all the turkeys on this trip. Gobble-gobble.

You were drinking with him.

A Cinzano. The beer's lousy. Besides I learn something about the place.

I'll bet. He's obsessed with women.

Naah!

He is too. I saw you watching them go by.

Rating them.

What?

Rating them.

What do you mean?

You know. Ten is the top of the line. Probably spill your drink. One is the bottom. Not worth looking up from the table. Most were in the four to seven range. Wrong neighborhood, Claude says.

Winthrop. You are sixty-seven years old!

So what?

Well I never. You don't look — rate in Toledo.

There's nothing to rate in Toledo.

Good thing our children can't hear you now.

The children couldn't care less.

I suppose you rated that Carleton woman high.

Never bothered.

Hah!

Hah what?

Never mind. How do I rate?

Right at the top.

You are the biggest liar I ever met.

You said your friend Alice was.

She doesn't know the difference.

I should have guessed.

Hurry up. Don't forget the camera.

I'm coming. Meet you in the lobby.

Winthrop — the bus is honking. Everybody's getting on. They'll leave without us.

Nobody's that lucky.

You're here. Where's the camera?

Damn! I left it in the room.

Oh God — go get it. I'll tell Madge to tell the driver. She talks French.

You call that French?

Winthrop, hurry.

We don't have to have the camera every day.

We can't leave without it.

Only the Japanese are required to bring cameras.

Winthrop!

O.K. But this is it. I knew I shoulda' stayed put. When we get back to Toledo I'm going to sit on the swing on the back porch 'til I rot. My new retirement plan: sit and rot I don't ca…If anyone says the word tour, cathedral, museum, gallery, Europe, airplane, bus — and especially bus! I'll kick butt all the way to Cleveland!

Winthrop! You are shouting. Everyone can hear you.

> *next to of course god america i love*
> *you land of the pilgrims and so forth —*

e. e. cummings

CRUTCHER

Warm for October first. One hundred five at that cemetery
in northern Sonora. The mexican caretakers nowhere in
sight as I walk around the oval drive that frames the graves.
A sprinkler set me running past the cut at the southwest
turn known as "infant's corner". I make another turn
northeast and there is an old man at his wife's grave. I'm
sure it's his wife without thinking about it twice. His car
waits forty feet away. The X of suspenders on his back over
a muslin shirt seems to have been branded on him years
ago. His face a chunk of boulder I cannot read. Crutches
on the ground beside him. He looks like one who would
drive his car long after his driver's license has been
cancelled. Law abiding but don't mess with his dignity, his
sense of self. The flat white hair on the back of his head
above the neck, has gone to ringlets in the heat. On one
knee, bent forward, he mumbles, remembering something
he forgot to tell her, or is telling her again — as if words
could penetrate the earth.

I keep moving, hearing bits of what he says. Asking for forgiveness. Hearing sorry. Sorry. Something about during the war. Forgive him for the malaria. Malaria had put him into the hospital in Manila where he met Senta. His mind had shut down. She spent hours nursing him. He would seize up with fear when she vanished at night. In the morning she reappeared and his heart began to run when he saw her violet, magnificent eyes. He belonged to her for months and when she got transferred out he grew weak again. So angry at everything he swung a sledgehammer at a jeep and couldn't make a dent. He had been forced into a part of himself he had never known. Malaria. It was the damn malaria.

How much of this have I really heard? Enough to fill in the blanks. When I come around to him again, he is off his knees and has started back toward his car. Sort of. A green, going rust grungy Styrofoam cemetery vase tucked under an armpit between crutch and ribs. He is moving slowly, almost imperceptibly, head down, laboring, determined, the only upright figure against the blue smear of the McDowell mountains behind him. I figure he is going to reach his car by sundown. I turn away and move toward the exit wondering if the nurse ever wrote to him. Then wonder why I wondered that. Why did I think her name was Senta. I couldn't have been close enough to know that could I? I walk a little faster, grateful the sun is hugging me.

After a minute I look back to check his progress but he is

down, nearer the car than I thought possible. I start to run to him but he sees me almost at once and I stop. He begins the effort to rise and one arm flailing like a troubled swimmer waves me off.

He has fallen before.

A FEW WEEKS

"How long will you be gone," she said. "Not long", he replied, "a few weeks." She looked at him as if she knew him well and forever. He said a few weeks like other people said a few hours. He would send her a card and a letter, she knew that, and of course he would bring her something. Other men went fishing and hunting. When he didn't have to, this one went just to be going. Another kind of woman could have shot him then and there. She was not like that.

He couldn't figure it out. When he was with her a part of him wanted to be moving on. Drawn to some elsewhere. When he was away from her he missed her. Talked about her, especially to Ruiz, his Mexican friend. "My Mexican," he would say, as if the black haired one belonged solely to him. The two of them roaring around the Federal District half in the bag, the car lurching through streets, waves of cantina music in and out of their open windows. Men and women leaning up against peeling doorways, looking like they've got no place to go and couldn't care less. Old people shuffling barefoot up a hill. Run-down buses with gold and silver chains and crucifixes swinging from sun visors. Scarves embroidered in a map of Mexico. Vendors hawking nearly every useless thing imaginable. Chickens in cages. A burro with a homemade cloth sign saying "Taxi" slung over his rump. People on bicycles swamped under loads of lamps or wood or pottery. Skinny perros lapping water from a sewer drain. Humanity everywhere.

The serious drinking lay ahead of them in Cuernavaca, or in the night, up in the cold hills above the city. Until morning, when Maria de los Angeles brought scrambled eggs to him and her boy husband, tending to their ills as if she were esposa to both. In the night she had gone away and they talked about their women with a confidential pride. Take a pull on whatever wasn't empty, passing it back and forth continuing. Two beauties out of different cultures. Maria's high cheekbones and angularity suggesting Maya or mestizo. Her alabaster skin against black eyes and black hair stunning. The gringa was the one with the unbelievable mouth and breasts like apples of ivory. Compare? Imposíble. Muy dificil one of them would say. Muy dificil, said the other, to no point anyone cared about. Then again louder, amigos spilling and going blind and deaf in the hint of sunrise.

He wrote her about Ruiz and his big ebony eyes set in pools of bloodshot liquid. And of Maria and the yellow and green cigarette case with no top and a mirror on the back she gave him in farewell. She wrote him about the children and the weather. When he got back he told her some of his life there. She said little. After one or two questions she acted like he had never left.

> *Poor Mexico, so far from God*
> *and so close to the United States.*
>
> Porfirio Diaz

BOBBY LOWELL AND ME

A girl is singing about Bobby Frost. First the music is slow and he is Robert. Then the tempo changes to jazzy finger snapping and he becomes Bobby. The concept and lyric is clever. I just don't remember much of it. In a fragment that I do, she asks him to write her a poem and not worry about dishpan hands. I'm hearing it but all I see is old Frost on television, reading and freezing in front of the Capital at Kennedy's inauguration. It is hard to think of Frost as Bob let alone Bobby. He seemed to have a hard edge to him and was said to have found bitterness in his old age. The sort of guy who might expect his juniors to call him Mr. Frost.

I begin to wonder if Lowell had ever been a Bobby too. The Robert or Bobby I read more intensely and devotedly was Lowell. Except I only knew of him as Robert. Or perhaps Robert-In-Desperation. All one name. I followed him as the young prophet of *Lord Weary's Castle* to the aging, introspective diarist of *Day by Day*. Often he could

41

not make poetry. There was Lowell the disillusioned, Lowell the uninspired, Lowell the madman in and out of institutions, wanting to say what happened, praying for accuracy. In *The Dolphin,* a book of earthly grace, he accepts responsibility for all his art and life, for all that his eye has seen and his hand has done. In his last book he had prophesied:

> *I will leave earth*
> *with my shoes tied*
> *as if the walk*
> *could cut bare feet.*

And he did. Soon after, riding in a taxicab from Kennedy Airport toward his home. September 12, 1977. On that day I was in Manhattan. In a coffee shop when the news came, as it usually does for me, over a radio. Just a few people in there, but I was still the only one who looked up. It was all over the papers coming out that afternoon and even some of the people on the indifferent streets spoke of it. "Robert Lowell died today," I told the doorman at a posh hotel, the urgency in my voice suggesting his passing was a danger to us all. "Who the hell is he?", he said. "He's the owner of this hotel," I said, hoping he would begin to fret about his paycheck. I was already tired of people dying wherever I happened to be. de Gaulle when in France. Stevenson in London. Another Pope in Italy. Now Lowell in New York, with Lennon coming up. Even Franklin Roosevelt died on my radio at home. A woman passing by our house just then also heard him go, spilling her groceries all over the sidewalk. It wouldn't end.

Sometimes chummy doesn't seem to work. A duck named Donald is not Don. James Bond is never Jim. Rhett Butler's real first name was Mister. And if you were Frost or Lowell, believe me, your name was Robert.

Poetry is the most dangerous game and the best

James Dickey

MAID SERVICE

Do you need the room now?

No. I just forgot something.

I'm almost finished.

No hurry.

I've seen you here before haven't I?

Could be. I've been here before.

Do you want the bed turned down?

No, that's O.K.

Do you travel a lot?

A lot.

I'll bet you get bored with it.

Just tired. Never bored.

Doncha' ever get lonely?

Sure.

I would get too lonely. I'd be lost without my cats.

Cats help.

I'll betcha' got girlfriends in every town. A lot a guys do.

Lot of guys make all that up.

Did ya ever bop a maid?

Excuse me?

Ya know. Have sex with a maid?

I don't think so.

My cousin says it happens all the time over in Houston.
But of course there's more places there.

Sure.

I almost took it from behind when I was cleaning a
bathtub. I was so surprised I screamed. A person oughta'
know when it's coming ya know.

Of course.

We're not supposed to mess with the guests anyway. It's
against their policy or somethin'.

It usually is.

I've never been really asked, ya know.

No. I didn't know.

My boyfriend wouldn't like it anyway.

I guess not.

Anyway who's got the time. They want us to run from room to room around here and we're always short help besides.

Well, I've got to get going. I just came back for this envelope.

Maybe I'll see you tomorrow.

I'm checking out tomorrow.

Yeah. I guessed you was.

MIDNIGHT CATHEDRAL

Every time Tal and I came to that town we had to look for
him. Pol. The big expatriate Dutchman with the handlebar
moustache. When we first met him he was in Amsterdam.
Said he didn't live there either. That one was the biggest
club he had. Pol's musichal — the last L missing. You
could even dance there. Then he moved to Brussels, in
increments smaller and smaller. But where? We had to find
someone who knew. Someone knew. It's over on
Clemenceau now, the someone said. Just look for a place no
one else would want in a dungeon full of blue smoke and
you'll be there. Finally, he lit for awhile, three years at least.
Rue de Stassart Twenty-Three a — Bruxelles, according to
my membership card. Pry the handleless front door open
and go downstairs. Walk through a narrow, sickly pea green
hallway to a slightly more welcoming entrance. On the
walls, signed photographs of the latest U.S. Air Force
Thunderbirds. Besides jazz, Pol loved pilots. The story was
he had been the first dutch member of the Royal Air Force
during the war. When he decided you were no longer a

stranger, he was benign. His legs had been damaged and he would come at you slowly, like a turtle. When he got to you or you to him, he would start to grin. "I'm lucky to be going so slowly because I may be going in the wrong direction." Then laughter all around.

I go in one night and there's no one at the bar, they're all standing near the band, watching a singer. Pol didn't have singers, except when the band sang and we sang with them. Something's up because it's à capella and even the band is amused. An exotic woman looking like a revolutionary in a cape or drape, it couldn't have been a dress, is passionately enchanting the house. In English, then French and back to English again, she is singing about a man she once loved and how she lost him and is going to move to Paris because Paris is the only town to get old in. If he shows up she is going to kill him; it will be good medicine for the sadness. To cheers and standing applause, she jumps off the stand and heads for the door. I never see her again. Pol comes out of his back office to all the tumult and says he doesn't have a clue. Sometimes it was that kind of place.

Tal was a busy guy, always running here and there trying to do three things at once. At Pol's he wrote his postcards. Pull the addresses from his jacket pocket and go to work. Girl friends, ex wives, colleagues, who knows. He even got me doing it a time or two. Usually he would write on the breaks, but not always. One night he was out of cards and wrote on the back cover of "POL's NEWS" a "MENSUEL

ORGANE du FRIENDS OF JAZZ." "You going to try and mail that?" I asked. "Sure," he said, "Let's see what happens", with a self assurance that always marked him. It was difficult to write. The small surface barrelheads that passed for tables made me put my drink on the floor. If the music was zippy I seemed to turn out a happy, breezy card. If the band was playing something like *In the wee small hours of the morning"*, slow and painful, it turned out melancholy or I couldn't finish it. By the time we got out of there, we would be too tired to write and it would literally be the small hours of morning.

The music was eclectic. Something Strayhorn did for Ellington was followed by a Swedish composer trying out some fugue for quintets. Towards closing time, or scream time as it came to be known, instead of thinning out, the crowd got thicker. Even ladies of the night, work done or plain worn out. Two or three at a time, sometimes more. Sit together or drift around the room. Pol didn't care. They needed music too, he said, and left it at that. The attraction was a last drink and the ding-dong lay 'em in the aisles closer, *"I scream, you scream, we all scream for ice cream"*. Bedlam every time. Everyone clapping, singing, standing, dancing in place, jumping up on the barrel tables, screaming, laughing, beaming and not wanting it to ever end.

Her name was Annie Dumont and she was a strumpet. At least that's what Tal called her at first. Others just called

her a hooker or they called her ennui Annie because she
seemed bored most of the time. I knew better. That look
was not boredom. She was lonely. That deep loneliness that
lies beneath the surface in the corners of the eyes and
sometimes spreads to the set of a chin. They hadn't really
seen her. Her hair had the color and cut of straw but not
the feel of it. Coal eyes with lashes you think impossible,
but they are hers. She is supple and graceful except when
she goes to sit. Then she throws herself down like a
schoolgirl in a tiff. Annie was nearly a regular; she loved the
charged atmosphere and the music. Sometimes she would
have a drink with us. Sometimes she would just stand and
peer over our shoulders when we did the postcard gig. One
night we can tell she is interested in playing at this so we
ask her if she wants to write a card. She has that look that
says, I thought you'd never ask. We put her between us and
Tal gives her a card. She works a long time crowding the
words in a cramped hand. We ask her who she is writing
to. Her brother Etienne. Where does he live. Paris. She
finishes and we offer to mail it for her. She is delighted. It
seems as though she has never done this before. It is close
to scream time and she hasn't moved. When it comes she is
transformed. On her feet, possessed like the rest of us,
grabbing our arms, trying to dance, laughing, her face
radiant. When it ends a rashness overpowers us. A kind of
madness. The kind that seizes you in a delirious moment
and hangs the consequence. Let's not mail the card to
Etienne, we said, let's go see him! Now. We don't even
think about it. Annie is ecstatic. The cab ride to the airport
is full of plans and silliness. No airplane until seven a.m., so
we sit at a concourse cafe bar sipping coffee with a

croissant. We find space on a DeHavilland Comet bound
for Orly and then on to Belgrade. Once on board I am still
wired and say we should stay on and go to Belgrade. Tal
just looks at me. The Comet complains and whines, but the
three of us fall asleep in seats meant for two, all tangled in a
knot. We arrive and passport control is giving us trouble.
No papers, no luggage, just a driving license. It never even
occurred to us. Annie goes to a ladies room and Tal to a
phone. He is always on the phone. I drink a cognac. Tal
won't drink in the mornings, he is usually sensible. Annie is
gone a long time. Tal comes back and we decide we may be
stuck. Finally, back comes Annie, looking down, she has
been crying. Then more tears. Annie look at me, I say. We
think we know what has happened, but we cannot bring
ourselves to say anything. Then the confession. The card
she wrote was to nobody. Bogus. There is no Etienne.
There never was an Etienne. And no one else for her in the
City of Light. A fantasy. An empty wish and a call for
attention answered by two screwy Americans. When we got
back, after all the apologies and tears and regrets, thank you
anyways and what the hell let's do it again sometime — we
slept forever. And then we left town, as we always did,
never knowing what happened next. There would come a
time with Tal when we would howl with laughter in
recollection. It was delicious. The whole wild crazy scene
was delicious.

And now? As for Annie who could say. I hope she is in a
fairy tale. A princess on the Avenue Foch dripping with
jewels. In my dream her eyes are dry, she is unpainted and

barelegged with her own child to keep. Tal, no doubt, is somewhere on a phone. I don't know whatever became of Pol. Like Ronnie Scott and others who ran our midnight cathedrals, he is probably dead. And the ice cream hymn? Maybe the next one up in somebody's stack of charts. In London town or old Bombay. For me it was in another life and I haven't heard it since.

KINGDOM

San Francisco. Table for two. Miss Peggy Lee has just
come out all in white. What the angels sing they learn from
her. Except for us the room is empty. The rest of the
country stands outside, waiting to get in. I love her madly.
You know it, knowing I love you more.

*

Ghirardelli Square. We are drawn to love in the afternoon.
But we stay too long — drunk on chocolate — barely able
to walk away. I wonder if we can have our stomachs
pumped. No food is worth what I am going to miss. Back
at the Top of the Mark, a first. Falling asleep before we can
get it on.

*

Twilight on the train near Santa Barbara. We watch a girl
and boy beginning to make love before a plate of fries. She

puts one near his mouth, making him reach, then pulls it back in the nick of time. She teases and he snaps like a dog, the game of keep-away continuing until he holds her wrist, winning; a kiss to her lips the real prize. They will forget the moment — and each other. It is we who will remember.

*

The fog in San Diego is so thick I nearly put us in Mission Bay. Another few yards and…Even the natives quit driving. I love the possibilities in your silence. You are just *there* like a shadow. The men who thought they loved you must be exhausted. In the dining room, two waiters are in a hushed squabble over which one will wait on you. When they look I whisper nothing in your ear, claiming you in public. They should have known. A few minutes ago I clasped your necklace. Slipped your buttons back into their holes, wistful, the way a man tells the world he doesn't want to.

*

Resting. Warmed by your hip pressing me. Rubbing my shoulders your idea. If you stayed with me because of the children, you would not bother. This week, all else at arm's length, is the Kingdom I've been restored to.

*

One breast now smaller than the other. The scar a slice and an omen. I hear apology. They cut what you said was mine. For a long time you were a dropped-wing bird in a cage. Our Father who art in Heaven, let all things go free that have survived.

LET ME CALL YOU SWEETHEART

I got a letter from a dead man. It had been sent to a hotel in Europe where I had been staying but I had moved on. Written in January and returned insufficient postage to the States in April, but I didn't know this yet, because it was still March and he was in an intensive care unit forty feet away. Just dead a few minutes. The letter was about his granddaughters and the National Football League. He said he had appointed himself my sportswriter and would keep me up to date. Written in a strong hand, there was not a word about his bad ticker or the woman he had buried nineteen months earlier. For a long time, I wished the post office had lost it; years later I couldn't seem to lose it either.

By the time I got to him he was or seemed semi-conscious, eyes closed, couldn't or wouldn't talk. Just squeezed my hand. Then I was sent to a family waiting room; two doctors urgently moving me — nearly strong-arming me away. No other patients or visitors around. As if on this late night, the place had been kept open, like a store waiting for a customer who said he was coming in. Unnaturally quiet. No nurses, orderlies or shift maintenance. Not even the hope of a radio playing or a swinging door, just a few crunched coffee cups abandoned by daytime death watchers. Then the speaker system went — Code Blue — or whatever it said, someone pell-mell down the hall with the wires and the paddles — my own heart in my throat, trying to get out. The jump-start cart never near the patient. When doctors one and two come out, I could have told them what they were telling me.

If this future, which has arrived, had been told by tealeaves, he would have nodded, to be polite, maybe so. Then insisted, God's hand was in it too. For a long time I looked out the window at the snow falling under the lights of the bridge that led back to the downtown. At the end of the bridge was the street where a car had struck him many years before. And a little further down, the railroad office where he spent so many years, almost Dickensian in its darkness, lights always on so they could see what they were doing. I forced myself to see it, knowing its exact location — him coming out of his gaol and boarding a streetcar that would carry him to a residential neighborhood. First a pause at the grocery, then the four block walk, heavy tall bags hiding all but his lively step. The women in the house timing the arrival of their protector.

It was perhaps one of those evenings he must hurry —
supper a donut dunked in coffee, all the hot liquid knocked
back in one motion as though he were a toper. Then off to
prepare for a minstrel show — Voilà! — we have a hobo —
where did he get that rig, unshaven, thoroughly dirty,
stained with facepaint, wearing a tattered overcoat only a
poseur would wear. Ready to leave. Offering a good night
kiss to his aged mother, who laughing and refusing, thanks
him, saying she will take his word for it. Leaving. A cigar
in one hand, stage shoes in a brown paper bag in the other.

Or another, slower, languid evening. Cribbage. Drumming,
humming and song. Always that. A songbook in his head.
Let Me Call You Sweetheart. I don't remember him calling
her that. He would sing a few lines to her and she would
coax him into another chorus. Music of Jerome Kern or
Hammerstein or another of those who wrote for Broadway.
Their era. She would gaze at him, eating it up, still arrested
by his agreeable romantic simplicity.

I tried to remember where I parked my car. I tried to
remember if I understood him very well. When I was
younger we were rarely on the same page. Years had gone
by before I realized it didn't matter if I understood him or
not. All I had to do was love him. I did know he got what
he could out of living. He knew a full life meant having
passions, fire. Like his ace contemporary Harry Truman, he
had done his damndest. Now I had to go and put him

down next to his wife. He wouldn't mind that part — he could go and find her. I think I knew all along it was the sum of him that mattered. Every man dies. Not every man really lives.

FIRE IN THE SKY

"She may not come Max. I don't think she wants to." The waitress at the Churchill kept bringing me sugared coffee and I kept sending it back.
"Look dummy, she hasn't seen you in a month and besides all dames love to shop," he laughed, whacking my shoulder. Then shook his head. "Relax," he said. "You don't even know your own wife."
"Small wonder," I said, fishing in my pocket for tip money, dollar or sterling didn't matter.
"What time you need to be at Heathrow?"
"I'll get a cab, Max."
"Yeah, I forgot. You prefer it. You're a weirdo."

They told her not to come. Her mother. The airline. Anybody who knew she was planning to leave. It wasn't safe. Miami was burning. If they were that concerned, I never understood why they just didn't cancel the flights. I was already there, having arrived a couple of days earlier.

Miami Beach actually. In the relative safety of the Doral Hotel. She came anyway. Said she was going to her husband and that was that. Which surprised me. I didn't think she cared that much anymore. Other things occupying her. Not much interest. Steamed about this or that. My continued absence had not made the heart grow fonder. Why she stayed married I never figured out. She was miraculous.

Before, when she had called to say she was on her way, I worried some. Sat on the edge of the bed staring at the phone. Then I went into the bathroom and stared at the toothbrush, shaving cream, lotion, thinking nothing, not seeing what I was looking at. If it wasn't the same with us, why did we seem to worry about each other sometimes. I thought I would never understand the flow of marriage and wasn't about to try. Others understood. My father did, I thought, but he was stable. His demons, if any, invisible. Then the old bad taste — marriage was an unnatural state. People bought into it because it was the path of least resistance and a consolation. I snorted at myself and went downstairs. Restless. Watched the people coming in and out, sometimes a couple arm in arm. Then the thought came of what a thin edge of life a man lived on without his own woman.

I could see the fire in the sky from the window of my room. It was miles off but I knew it was serious stuff, not as bad as the press said, yet it had the potential to get worse.

When I went out on the street I could smell it. Back in the lobby a rumor passed that the nearby Fountainbleau had been selected for the torch. The day after she arrived, the hosts of the conference I was attending, beaming with new authority, informed us we were not to leave the "Hotel Row" area on the beach and venture across Biscayne Bay into the city, unless we were registered for and riding in the Doral bus. While on one level this seemed melodrama, on another it made the whole scene even more romantic. I took to calling the roof garden restaurant and lounge *Rick's Café Américain*. For five days she simply moved the marriage bed from where she lived to where I was. Once in a while I would get up and slide into a meeting on the ground floor in one of those cavernous high ceiling conference rooms the older hotels have. More often I would not.

In late afternoon I watched her changing clothes, fixing her hair, her movements patient and deliberate as always. Except now she worried about everyone and the stack of years weighed on her making her look heroic and poignant. Daydreaming, I turned the clock back on us...

She liked mornings the best — in the hotels where room service brought croissants and marmalade. She could eat and have her juice and cream with a little coffee in it without getting fancy and going downstairs. Queen's breakfast. In Vienna, he had made a mistake in ordering for her, or room service had, and they brought dozens of eggs and loaves of fresh toast on a catafalque with wheels, enough for the royal Hapsburgs — and room enough for them too in her suite of fleshy splendor. He liked evenings the best — the darkness wakened him, the cities blazed beckoning him. In Paris, she had made a mistake in turning him onto a street she wanted to walk, seconds later swinging her umbrella, duelling away a persistent street walker of another kind who would compete with her. She was not amused, but he was, the inflated object of their riot. One would have him for money, the other for love and money. In the end paying up, he would, if they had made a truce, gladly fed them both...

We spent chunks of the middle day walking the shoreline of the Atlantic before scalding on blankets in the glare. Nothing said except to point out a nearby ship, guessing destination, or what might be an approaching squall, guessing landfall. Then dehydrated and hungry we hurried off to what passed for late lunch in the cool subterranean coffee shop — iced tea and ice cream. On our last full day, scanning the horizen, we both saw her at once. Though far out, the unique angle of the funnel was unmistakable. Nothing else like her. *Le pluslong pacquebot dans le monde* — the longest passenger ship in the world, her advertisements proclaimed. Charles de Gaulle's pride and joy, *The France* had been sold to Norway and now in a second life cruised the Caribbean. We were lucky to see her again, we said, lucky to have been on so fine a ship, even though it had been her second roughest crossing. The elegance, Sugar Ray Robinson dancing, French onion soup at three in the morning on a rolling, pitching sea. Some of the women passengers jealous because the Captain and his officers danced mostly with her. All of that and more.

It had been many years since we boarded her and returned to America. For a moment our yesterdays overwhelmed us. We looked at one another and laughed. Perhaps we could find a way out there and hijack her to Southampton. Then hide in the loo on the boat train to London. Or perhaps not. Sand snuggled between our toes. We could not make Miami spend the night alone. As if to do so would be thoughtless.

I've got the world on a string

Francis Albert Sinatra

JUST A FIGURE OF SPEECH

The man and woman have come to this desert with their two children, girls six and four, from Jersey, the isle off the British coast, reachable by air from London in about thirty minutes. I first saw them on a Saturday at the swimming pool, the better part of a good eye intent instead on their nearly perfect companion, sitting in a whirlpool or spa as it is sometimes called. Smiling back at me was a young version of Jacqueline Bisset, the bright sun detailing and confirming my memory. We spoke briefly before she climbed out, the water dripping from her reluctantly. She took her life and walked away, not showing off, not full of herself. She simply sat in a shaded lounger, her back to all of us, and began to read from a book.

After that the couple came without her — just the chattering girls jumping in and out of the water. The empty spa still and gloomy. The mother scolding me for not coming across to Jersey, when I had been in London and had surely had the chance. "Shame on you, if you don't," she said. "Must do," the husband added. "Look at me, Dadday," shouted the six year old. "Wotch me, Dadday," implored the other. Their words a required accompaniment to each jump into the water. Endlessly.

"Wotch them, Hector," the woman ordered.

Their presence has been disturbing. I do not want to talk to them. I have become accustomed to the August quiet, the time of year when it is too hot for tourists and most shops, hotels and pools are empty. The time of year when your whole body declares it's time for shoeless walks at midnight in a place where nobody else does. There is plenty of time in February and March for the shouts, the hurt feelings the tears and "just one more minute puhleeese!"

Later on, as the water began to drift into shadow and with the girls out of earshot, the man says to his wife; "When we get back, I'm going to screw you to death." That it is just a figure of speech indicating hunger and intensity, well at least intensity — usually not fatal — should be palpable, but I have only just met Hector. Sex as pure destruction. What happened to peace? Silence. Only the girls babbling to a blue haired granny who has just entered the water farther down, telling them not to splash her.

I am waiting for some reply, wondering what it is in this woman that makes the male rise in him. Whole afternoons seem to pass. I have decided she is ignoring him, when suddenly she says; "Will you raise the girls by yourself?"

SECRET AGENT

For as long as I can remember I wanted to be a spy.
Hollywood and the history of our time were inspiration.
When Bogart played Sam Spade it was close but no cigar.
The film was atmospheric and caustic cool but he was stuck
in one town. And he was a P.I. Then news of the
underground came; French, Dutch, Norwegian patriots
doing a number on the enemy at great risk, sometimes
getting shot or a slit throat for their trouble. Anecdotes
included a resistance girl who would hide a downed flyboy
in a haystack, until she could get him across some border.
Overtones that sucked you in. And there was Bogart again.
This time making a difference in foreign intrigue. That
most reluctant hero Rick, who loved Ingrid Bergman's Ilsa
Lund. Maybe it was those two won the war.

When my first chance came I turned it down. I could carry
something closed end. One trip, one drop. Good terms
spelled out quickly and carelessly by a "machinery salesman"

from the other side. Mercurial northern european. An oxymoron to some. Big. Round cuff links the size of silver dollars. In an Athens hotel bar where he could have easily been overheard. Not the smartest guy I met. More memorable was a shaded, tiresome strobe, blinking at the dull room, someone's idea of ambience. At first he had been chatty, then bored both of us with a little speech he had no real interest in. Somehow he had got the impression I was Canadian. Instead of checking out the next morning, I checked out that night and went to the airport.

I got discouraged and tended to my knitting for awhile. Couldn't get a length of hair to stick and stay between door and frame the way the pros did it. Couldn't photo memorize a bunch of numbers the way I thought you had to. Grew tired of looking for "bugs" in hotel rooms never touched. Still, I was a willing "Joe" with nobody to run me. I dismissed the idea I needed special training — couldn't get it anyway. Then it came to me where I was ripe for it and could have expected it. Central America. What I wouldn't do in Athens I would for a friendly. Simple courier. I couldn't resist. In that short period of time it was known I shuttled between countries by car. Packets I never dreamed of opening. Once, a jewelers envelope, so small it should have held a small chain for a child. Mostly, I was free from paranoia. Driving between Guatemala City and San Salvador, big rocks blocked the crummy road, making it temporarily impassable. I was sure it was an ambush, refusing to remember that interrupted travel was as much a rule as it was exception. There was no room with a single hanging lightbulb. No weapon, no false papers, no safe house. Just two or three contacts and occasionally a message from a messenger I never saw. I received payment-in-kind; generous quantities of Ballantine scotch and hard to get american cigarettes. And the adrenaline rush that came with the doing.

Agent days over, I had one more brush up against it. The Bolshoi Ballet had come into Santo Domingo from Havana. So unexpectedly early their hotel rooms were not ready. The troupe apparently worn out. Slept curled or spreadeagled on lobby furniture or strewn like dead bodies on the steps of an open, circular stairway. Not one of them appeared to be awake. Their luggage stood in clumps all over the place. Only the KGB were alive. Standing at attention. One by the desk looking out, one by the front door looking in, one by the staircase looking at me, maybe more. I bent to examine the luggage, at first casually, then more closely when I see this annoys KGB. I look for tags, names, cities, stickers, anything, aware there may be nothing I can read. KGB staircase moves toward me, but I keep it up, playing him. When he gets to me and stops I rise and face him. He glares at me. I glare back. Nothing is said. Then I turn on my heel and go up to my room. As the elevator climbs, I imagine I have flattened him and the other goons. The sleeping dancers have come awake and are applauding, the building exploding with their sound. The next day, of course, they will all defect to the west.

Over the years, John le Carré came along and showed the underside of the spy game. The treachery, the disillusion and abandonment. That said, he didn't take the magic out of it. Nobody did. If you were born to be a secret agent you never quite got over it. How could you, if the word espionage was more seductive than any perfume. How could you, if you loved smoky saloons, airplanes with propellers and nutty dames.

STILL RAINING

It had started to rain around seven o'clock and each hour
after that it seemed to rain a little harder. Now it was past
midnight and it was raining harder than ever. And he was
soaked through. He wished, too late, he wasn't out in it. He
had insisted on walking, giving up the ride that would have
kept him dry. Had told the people he was with that he liked
walking in the rain. He did unless the rain came with wind.
What he didn't tell them was, he would rather be wet than
listen ad nauseam to more business talk. It would have
meant another hour of high pitched elitist superiority,
spilling drinks on each other, complaining about the service
the locals gave, calling it the mañana disease. Banal bullshit.
Still, he could have had a taxi. He had come to where his
hotel was two short blocks away, but he just stood there
watching the girl across the street. She just stood there too,
like him, getting wetter, water rolling off an old floppy hat
onto her soaking shoes. No coat, a little purse on her wrist
below a short sleeve dress. Nothing going for her in this

weather, he thought, nothing going for her at all by the look of her. After a few seconds, she held up one leg a little, then the other, like a dog that wants to come inside, tired of cold wet paws. He started to move toward the hotel, then feeling he was abandoning her, reversed himself and hurried across the street and stood beside her. For a moment, she didn't even look up. She was shivering, absolutely drenched and, he thought frightened. Finally she tried to smile and failed, her eyes blank, defeated. "C'mon. Adelante," he said, "let's get out of here. Vamanos." She gave no sign of moving. As if moving meant she would drown. He reached and gently lifted the rim of the floppy hat and kissed her wet nose. "You will be O.K.," he said, "come with me." He took her by the hand and pulled and she started to walk like she had no choice.

When they entered the lobby, the night clerk didn't bother to lift his head to them. In the elevator he realized he had not let go her hand, that she was slightly more relaxed, holding his hand tighter, as if she were hopeful or had begun to trust. As soon as he unlocked the door she went into the bathroom and got out of her clothes. When she came out she had on one of those hotel robes, much too large, her head sticking out as through a tent. She was still dripping so he slid by her and got a towel and started to dry her hair. She gave a short laugh, the only one, taking the towel from him, wanting to dry herself.

"Que es su nombre?," he asked.
"No." she answered.

"No? No es su nombre?" he said, trying to cheer her up. "No hablamos, ahora no. Por favor," was all she would say. When he thought about it later, he realized that was all she had said. He sat in a chair wrapped in a blanket watching her, his wet clothes laying where they fell, shiny against the bone dry floor. On the bed, legs folded, feet sole to sole, she dried her hair for awhile and dropped the towel onto her lap, sighing. She pulled the robe off and let it fall around her, as if it had been wrong to put it on at all. His eyes gathering her stopped at large, blue and amber welts on her shoulder and stomach. She resumed drying her hair. Then perfectly still, the towel put aside, looked at him for a long time, not a hint of a word forming, appraising him, imagining who he was or not thinking of him all. He could see a little life in her eyes now, her guard falling with the robe. She didn't look anything like the wet girl in the street, in the hat, dress and heels. Somebody's daughter. Maybe somebody's mother. Just not the wet, troubled girl in the street. And she wouldn't talk.

She moved away from him to brush her hair. He stayed put just waiting. Drying. He thought about her childhood and that of others in the shadow of the city. The kid who would guard your parked car for a few pesos while you were away — and if you didn't pay him — might be the same one who slashed the tires. Was more than that out of reach? Perhaps they are waiting for the next life, believing dimly, not in heaven exactly, but a place where they can talk together quietly, or at least their spirits can, unafraid, away from randomness where there is plenty and hurts are healed. Or it is all a bad joke, there is nothing on either side of the door and not worth thinking about. Was she dismayed to always find the apple offered her just a core? Had she at her pubescence been the first one pushed out the door? Just when he wondered why it takes so long to brush hair, she came back.

For a long time she had clung to him as if he were a last hope. Then she fell asleep. On her right side pressed up against him exchanging heat. He listened to the rain and her breathing, sorry and not sorry he had brought her with him. She had pulled his left arm across her and tucked the hand under her breast, locking it there as she slept. He could feel his hand going to sleep, but knew he wouldn't move it. Soon he would be asleep himself.

When he woke it was late morning and before he opened his eyes he knew she was gone. There was no surprise in that, just curiosity. If she had made a sound he hadn't heard it. He sat on the edge of the bed, a trace of their aroma lingering on him, the room appallingly barren. Fighting off wondering where she went. From habit he pulled open the nightstand drawer always expecting to find a bible. Instead he found her bracelets. When had she put them in there? He didn't know. The painted red and yellow swirls in isolation seemed pathetic. Something about finding them made him worry about her. He slammed the drawer and rubbed his eyes not wanting to get dressed. He didn't have to turn and look out the window. He could hear it. It was still raining.

QUATROCENTENARIO

Cane got off the plane at Maiquetia where the runway apron nearly touched the sea, greeted by familiar humidity and the hundreds that looked like thousands coming out of the hill barrios to watch arrivals and departures. They were always there, day or night; he wondered what else they did. Delgado wouldn't be meeting him this time and Gustavo was on business in Maracaibo. He would get a taxi and go up through the Avila into the city alone. He liked going into cities by himself. There was an excitement or anticipation in doing it that way that was blunted if someone accompanied him. Before they pulled away he knew exactly when it would be on the steep slope of the Autopista that the humidity would begin to drop and his ears would pop from the change in altitude. He had been on the road a lot this year, a little much again, especially here, the third or fourth time if he remembered right. If it wasn't for the marvelous Hotel Tamanaco and the big birthday bash he might have…

Quatrocentenario. Caracas was four hundred years old. A year long birthday party under way. Mardi Gras above the Caribbean. Soon he would see the city and look at the Avila from another direction. From anywhere on the grounds of the hotel, he could see the hill's changing expression, a hue that went from sandy-gold to bright green and when the sky was overcast, violet. The city was the usual traffic snarl. Celebration couldn't change that. He wondered what it looked like when a Spanish captain, Diego de Losada arrived and founded the city of Santiago de Leon de Caracas. Did Losada have the benefit of the Bougainvillae and their pink, lilac and white petals and the shiny flowers of the yellow Poui tree? Maybe he had more. If no, thought Cane, he missed the most enchanting bouquet in South America. Cane could smell them in his sleep He checked into the hotel and turning to look for the porter round Gustavo standing there instead, white teeth shining, briefcase, as always, in hand.

"Hey man! I thought you were in Maracaibo."

"Hey Buddy, Welcome. I got back late this morning. Don't like that place. The plant stinks. You said it yourself. Don't forget Buddy, I am a Caraqueno. Come on." They walked through a large, lavish lobby, back outside of a garden patio bar, half indoors half out, weaving through crowded luncheon tables under sun umbrellas, trees and flowers everywhere, put down by oil money that drenched the country's rich. They sat and ordered drinks. Cane looked down at Gustavo's briefcase with the colt .45 automatic inside.

"Gustavo you shoot anybody while I was gone?"

"C'mon Buddy, that's my protection. Safety first, you know

that.'" "Bloody shame," Cane waved him off. "You can't even go to the can without that thing." Gustavo was a lawyer. An abogado with enemies was the way he put it. "Cheers Buddy," Gustavo said.

"Cheers."

"Delgado says Pablo Cane is not your real name."

"Where is Delgado?"

"Miami. Delgado is always in Miami. Cuban relatives. Girlfriends. So why Pablo Cane. What kind of a name is that?"

"Half Spanish, half Irish, I guess. I got it out of a book." Gustavo is laughing.

"What was the matter with your born name?"

"I didn't get to choose it."

"You're loco, Buddy, you know that. But it's great to see you. Drink up." Gustavo swept up his glass and emptied it. "We should be finished downtown by six. Get back here before all the parking is gone."

It is after seven and Cane is in his room cleaning up. Music fills his space as though he were already downstairs. The poolside orchestra is the nearest. He can look down from his open window and see them. There is another in the ballroom. A small combo plays in the lobby. Gustavo is already waiting for him there. A cigar, no doubt, half gone. Cane thinks Gustavo is almost a professional voyeur. "You just watch tonight, Buddy," he said on the way back to the hotel. "You will see some of the most beautiful women in the world." "And you will play with most of them," Cane said. "No, too many are adolescente."

"When did that ever bother you, amigo?"

"C'mon Buddy, give me a break." Cane had observed the ladies man in him when they first met. The way he talked about them and to them. Gustavo was not obsessed with the entirety of women; he was obsessed with what in each one he had not had, with the smallest part that makes one woman different from another. Even then, Cane thinks, something is nearly always withheld. He is reluctant to go downstairs. He has seen all this before. In one form or another, in cities everywhere. It repeats itself in his mind's eye. A girl has already drank too much and is falling out of her high heels. A young man is so aroused he is embarrassed to stand up and dance. Hell, he had grown up with it. He would rather see it from his room. He knows instinctively that solitude has advantages that are more deeply satisfying than those of other conditions, but it is still difficult. He wants to join the party but he knows, once there, he will not see it as he sees it now.

Gustavo has already cornered a girl. His cigar ash is about to fall on both of them. By the time Cane reaches him she is saying goodbye. Gustavo would frown but he is too charming.

"What gives?"

"She is going downtown to the Hilton."

"Why?"

"She says the music's better."

"How would she know?"

"She doesn't. She needs to make an appearance at every party."

They check out the ballroom. Studs everywhere. They are bronzed and darkly handsome with tight fitting clothes. They look as if everything has been too easy, already weary of the gifts in beautiful gowns standing before them. Macho head to toe. Maybe they are entirely what they seem. Dancers grind into each other, inhibitions put aside. Others look self satisfied, convinced they have found the only path to paradise. A fierce, protective matron appears, chasing down one of the vulnerable daughters of the city. Cane sits there looking out. Looking and not seeing. His mind is on a woman three thousand miles away. He can see her in a robe brushing her hair and then coming up behind him, saying nothing as she begins to rub his shoulders for a minute. He remembers a time she liked to wash his hair, the feeling of her leaning into him, rinsing him, both of them bent over a sink, later toweling him, telling him she read somewhere such vigorous rubbing postponed baldness. He thinks of the time of the day and thinks she will be sleeping and then tries not to think of her anymore.

"Where you at, Buddy?," Gustavo interrupts. Cane just smiled. "At midnight we go outside and shoot our pistols." He pulls an imaginary trigger in the air. "Quatrocentenario. Everything goes."

"You coming?"

"Old Tucson in old Caracas."

"What?"

"Nothing. Thanks. You can tell me all about it tomorrow."

In the morning Cane thought of her again. In the middle of shaving. She would come to him like that, without warning. They were in Madrid. He had been at work while she and a friend had gone about the city. In the late afternoon they had been in a bus accident. The bus driver in a rage had simply walked away. When he returned to their hotel in early evening, he found the two of them sitting on the floor of the room laughing, dried blood stuck to their ruined nylon stockings. Later he had put her on the bed and washed the small cuts. One thing had led to another and they were in bed a long time. All this made them late for a dinner and they didn't care. He thought of her legs again and then tried not to think of her anymore.

"Tonight it's fireworks. Orgasms in the sky," said Gustavo, pleased with himself. "Is that so," Cane replied, only mildly interested. He was looking for a little more rest. The music had flooded him all night, alternately waking him and putting him to sleep. They had passed another day and this night went to the outdoor garden party. Gustavo said he had arranged to meet a girl in the lobby at ten o'clock and might be gone for awhile. Did his Buddy mind? Buddy did not mind. They sipped on Campari and watched tireless youth. Cane looked from left to right and back again. Beauty. Opulence. Absurdly regal decoration. In the middle of the grounds, in front of an elaborate waterfall, an ice sculpture of the Great Liberator, Simon Bolivar. Wealth and the appearance of wealth. A few Cinderellas he would rather know amidst their cinders. The beauty parlor and the dressmaker the providers of disguise. The orchestra paying no attention as though parties on this scale occurred all the time. Later, he walked alone around the edges of the evening. The Bougainvillae and the Poui trees assailing him again. A doorman tells him how coincidence brought a boy and girl together here after a forced separation. Except the doorman is certain it was fate. At the desk there was a message. "Buddy. I have gone with Madolina to her apartment. Not sure I will be back for fireworks. If not, I'll call you later. Find yourself a señorita. Gustavo." As he put the note in his pocket and looked up, a muchacha gorda just standing there winked at him. He winked back at her and walked away.

He is in his room again. Packing his clothes even though he is not scheduled to leave for two more days. He was nearly finished before he realized what he was doing. Then it came to him out of nowhere. He just wanted to be gone. Enough was enough. What was going on was frantic. None of this belonged to him or he to it. It was real, but it also wasn't. He needed simple. Just wanted to be away. He remembered where he had the milkshakes when he was in school. Had the soda girl who wore bobby socks and smelled of soap. That place where you could put your foot on the train track and feel the train coming before you ever heard or saw it. That place where all you have to do is walk up the driveway and the big dog is at the door looking out at you, waiting for you.

MEMENTO MORI

You've had everything at least once.

I know.

You can't expect it again. Memento mori.

I know.

You should be grateful. Some people never come even close to having the life you've had. As the saying goes, your cup runneth over.

I know.

The thing is, a lot never got through school, just had jobs kept them in food. Never left the county they were born in.

I know.

Some people gave themselves a beating and then quit. You know what it's like to win at things. Lose. Learn from losing and win again. Fall down. Get up. Fall again and refuse to stay down. Get up and move on.

I know.

People cared about you. Early and later on. Second chances. Third chances. Opportunity. That's what you had. Opportunity.

I know.

That German friend of yours took you to the red light district in Hamburg to meet a frau he knew, then got sidetracked, showing you bomb damage still unrepaired from the war. Got so angry at the yanks he said did it all and then decided you were responsible as well. Pulled a gun and said he was going to shoot you? How about that?

I know.

And what about the time that prop job blew both engines landing in Norway in a snowstorm. All of you so smashed on duty free booze they had to tell you about it afterward. Nobody shook up until they read it in the papers next day. Lucky sods all of you.

I know.

Those guys you knew who never lived to finish raising their own children, let alone ever see a grandchild. Could easily have been you.

I know.

If you died now, right this minute, you'd not have one damn thing to complain about.

I know.

Hell's the matter with you then?

I don't know.

HEROES

Here's to
those, easy to love, offed themselves overcome by living,
their world somehow out of hand. All their walls dark
corners.

Here's to
a small child still in diapers, a port catheter for intravenous
medication in his chest. At bedtime he tucks a ball under
his blanket and takes his chemotherapy pill. Acute
lymphoblastic leukemia.

To Eliana and Katie in Sienna of a summer noon. The
cobblestone reflecting red from Katie's new red shoes.
Eliana and Katie on top of the world, unknown that
moment but to themselves.

And a boy drummer hard at work on his new drum set. In the street below, a man begins to dance to all that banging, bowing to the dumb parked cars. Upstairs, the boy's mother, making beds, wiggles her hips.

Zapata
sowing trust, if the word fits. Renouncing power in the moment of victory. And Zapatistas I have known.

De Grazia
painting indians, angels without noses, black eyes perfectly set. Mouths nearly upside down little hearts. No victims. No judgments. Just Ted seeing what others didn't.

An old drunk, posing as a human, wakes to a new day, determined to try life again, blinking at the morning's awful and stupid clarity.

The town crazy, undaunted, half-wild, half-domestic, back and forth on errands only he knows the meaning of, looking sad in his worthy life yet suited to it. The town worried he has seen a truth no one can handle.

The cooks, stitchers, fasteners, inscrutable needle threaders, unopen, unillumined, unconditionally caring for us, never controlled their lives, never pretended they did, never questioning what it all amounts to or ever will.

The mismatched surrendered to the irreparable. Whatever is honorable settled for and settled into; the self that is repressed lives on its own, heartstoppingly, impossibly in love, in silence.

Here's to you, somebody's hero. If not in life, in death.

Let us honor if we can
the vertical man,
though we value none
but the horizontal one

W. H. Auden

THE SITTING ROOM

She wanted a space of her own:
a raggedy doll as mime
slumped against a wall
or limber-limbed doing splits
if it — and she — were happy.
A child's tea table with matching chairs,
little women and wild birds sipping tea.
A white cradle now a white ship
sinking under a heap of memorabilia;
a nightstar constant at her window
in the Sitting Room.

A place of patience
away from all that jazz and a husband
living among his selves —
a world he walked alone to every day
though it was not his anymore.

A place to hex imaginary mites.
Float in lapse-time. Disconnect.
Days over
humming through a mouthful of pins.

Sorry little difference, he thinks,
between pain and waiting for pain…

The unknowable burned in him.

BRAZILIAN RAIN STICK

Again I give you
Music we once never knew
To listen for. A slight turn

Of wrist gives a sprinkle of drops
Falling out of leaves. Upend the thing to
Drizzle or downpour, the turned for and the turner

Calmed. So what if it is seed
Or pebble in a stalk. You are
Like a rich girl entering heaven

After running through its scales.
My eyes plead
Get out of that sick bed and

Follow me to where they trap the rain
So we can get another
And another,

Brazil and this rain stick
Undiminished
If we have more of both.

ENDGAME

First reading mystery stories. Then working crossword puzzles. At last, not looking at me. Looking at the wall, holding beads, saying beads, not looking at me.

*

Even on oxygen her breathing is labored. I discover I have been holding my breath a lot. Guilty she can see me breathing on my own.

*

She is in the wheelchair. We register again. No. A supervisor comes and says forget it. They are waiting for us upstairs. They knew we would return.
Did anyone not know.
Transport will come and get her.
No. I am transport, I say.
I take her up myself.

I would take her through the roof. Back to France. Cap
d'Antibes. Stay until we found our lost life. Our lost lust.
On the beach drawing pubic triangles in the sand. Her
sweeping them away if someone comes along. The elevator
rises. My brain finally tells me we couldn't make it to New
York.

*

The endgame begins.
There are forms of farewell.

Tell me about the night we met.

I tell her what she already knows —

But

embellishing. Adding falsehood she knows is coming.
Bending close making sure she can read between my lines.
Making sure I get...oh God,

Approval.

*

The woman in the bed is a thousand years old.
The night we met, a thousand years ago.

THE COMFORT OF CERTAINTIES

"You want some coffee?"

" Sure — decaf."

"Decaf?," he sniffed. "You one of those tryin' to live forever." She just shook her head at him. He hadn't changed. He had known her since she was a girl and was at ease around her. Say any damn thing on his mind. The way you had a special pass with people you grew up with. A part of him looked like he had fallen out of bed and he hadn't bothered to straighten things up. Another part looked like someone who had once studied things he didn't want to learn and it had made him undisciplined and mischievous, a man gone into exile.

"I'm going to have another baby pretty soon," he said.

"Sure you are," she answered. Today he looked seventy-five. Easy.

"I am," he said.

"You mean your daughter is. Why do you keep telling people that. You're having delusions. Eventually that line wears thin."

"Not really. Some laugh but others look at me and the child I'm holding and wonder. I can see the change in their eyes as they realize it's possible. They think of some famous guy and then decide I might be another crazy old dude that's done it. Then when they are wavering on the line between doubt and belief, I look at them real hard and will them into a certainty."

"You're nuts," she said.

"No more than other people who tell you outrageous stuff, who don't know you or hardly do. Or you're related to them and they tell you anyway."

"Like what?"

"Like somebody will give you an opinion or hearsay but present it as fact. They'll say John Kennedy balled every woman who ever came within one hundred yards of the White House and then wait for you to agree with them. They don't have a clue. Or they repeat some common wisdom that a ten year old won't buy, all relaxed like they expect they are preaching to the choir. They are certain of everything."

"Can't be that bad."

"It's worse. Just listen to people when something tragic happens. They hear something from their minister or therapist and then word for word it back to you."

"Like?"

"Like it was God's will. You don't leave this world until your work is finished. And on and on. How the hell do they know?"

"People have to say something."

"No they don't. Or they could say tough luck Chico, better luck next time and leave out the platitudes."

"Don't be so hard on everybody. People need the comfort of certainty," she said, slowly releasing her grip on his arm. "They need to believe everything is taken care of."

"They're whistling in the dark."

She seemed tired and uncomfortable, sighing and crossing her arms in front of her. They were silent for awhile.

"Have you picked a name for that new baby?," she looked at him.

"Not yet," he grinned.

SOMEBODY ELSE

I came upon your diary from 1963. You were twenty-eight years old. I had forgotten how happy you were then. How much you enjoyed your everyday doings. Going off with French, Swiss, Swedish and American friends to simple pleasures. That you tasted acquavit but did not disclose your impression. Figures. How weather closed the Geneva airport and you waited up for my train to arrive at five A.M., both of us so tired we slept into the afternoon. Our Easter trip to Paris is there. The details of your ways. Cleaning your silver stoically. A fair price for the dinners you loved to give. How you bought yarn to knit a scarf for me. If I phoned you, you wrote it down. If I took you with me you wrote it down. I can almost see you tucking your legs up under you and telling me about your day.

I see you from a distance. It is hard to remember you then. We were somebody else.

HUSBAND

Too busy living large
I never knew
I loved the way
A woman says the words
My husband
Until I wasn't one anymore

MISSISSIPPI GOTHIC

He liked the natural displacements of things. The swayback
of an old horse. The greying muzzle of an old dog. The
random yet self determined way a dress falls to the floor
before a woman steps out of it. Felt the same about houses
and the land around them. They weren't interesting until
they reached maturity. Then they got better. Began to say
something of themselves.

The place was slowly falling apart. Had needed painting for
some time. Mortar from bricks attached to steps, first
separated, then vanished. Shrubbery untended. Animal
gravestone lost under weeds. Driveway cracked in the form
of a spider web. The roof would have sunk by now, but she
had asked him to replace it. It needed only a magnolia tree
and oppressive humidity to remind him of something he
had seen or read about. The old willow tree was a start.
Willows could be a premonition if you let them. Houses
like humans took wounds in similar ways. You could fix a

place on the outside, healing it to the eye and know that underneath the cosmetic little changed. What was the use of putting pancake makeup on an old broad — just make her look garish. When she is beyond repair, the details of her life, the weight of living, are a revelation not history to be rewritten. He worried that a makeover would be a kind of arrogance. Too much suggestion of life ahead taken for granted. It was up to the younger ones to do that. Sometimes older people made foolish assumptions, denying their possibilities narrowed down moment by moment.

It had been awhile since he worked all this. Younger man. Kids still at home. Big dog watching him intently, while he raked or trimmed or fixed, acting like it was a straw boss, making sure he did not slack off. Even then, he imagined in shirtless heat what all this would look like when the noiseless foot of time overtook it. He figured he was just borrowing it. Everyone up and down the street. They were all borrowers. Or maybe it was something else. Perhaps what he was looking at now was why so many moved into manageable apartments or condominiums. Or they simply set out for some counterlife, seeking distance and never returned. Perspectives changed. People in their lives who gave them pleasure and purpose had begun to march off without them.

As he turned to go inside, he saw a pickup pull up and stop. Dusty city truck with the emblem fading away. Heavy clicking sound from under the hood until the driver turned the ignition off. Has to slam his shoulder into the jammed door before he can get out. Walks into the yard slow and looking up into the sky like he'd rather be somewhere else, wearing a baseball cap that says American Legion Post something or other. When he stops and says "hullo," scar tissue moves around his face. Some kind of inspector. Pulls out his I.D., palming it upwards. "Name's McCall. Lotsa' neighbors worried about yer place. Isn't kept up. Think yer drivin' real estate down."

"Maybe. It's been on its own awhile."

"Looks like yer headed for Mississippi gothic," the Legionnaire said.

"What?"

"Goin' to seed. Sort of irrational. Desolation and decay. Mississippi gothic. William Faulkner stuff."

"This place isn't up to Faulkner standard."

"Well, I'm jus' doin my job. Here ta tell ya to get after it. S'pposed to follow up complaints."

He looked beyond McCall to the forlorn truck, then down to the ground, loving irony.

"Somethin' funny?"

"Everything's funny in a way."

"I gotta check back with ya in a month."

"Well, maybe one of these days I'll just burn the place down — give it a proper sendoff."

"Then you'll go to jail," the incredulous city man said, backing up in the direction of his truck. "This ain't Mississippi."

Life is what happens when you are busy making other plans

John Lennon

PRETTY WOMAN II

I thought I might rent one. Like Richard Gere did in
Pretty Woman. Women weren't banging at the door where
I lived and in the circumstances I was in, age and all — my
prospects weren't very good. Besides, if I rented a hooker
for a fixed period of time, say a week or maybe less, we
could do what I wanted. Of course I could buy her a flower
or take her to dinner, or both, or go to a movie. Something
like that. If I went about finding a woman in the
conventional way, I would have to do what she wanted —
go bowling, shopping, listen to her talk about her aunt
Mabel. After the first day or so, she would ask me not to
smoke around her, stop scratching and then ask why I had
to blow my nose. After I told her, she would ask how to
spell rhinitis. Then the real questioning would begin. Why
did I work at night and sleep in the morning. Sooner or
later we would get to how much money did I have. Why
couldn't we go see the pyramids of Egypt or somethin' just
as far away. The more I thought about it the more it
sounded like being doomed. More depressing, it would

make me think about me. I didn't want to think about me, I wanted to think about somebody like Julia Roberts.

The best way to get it done seemed to be to imagine it first. Work it out in the mind, even dream parts or all of it, if possible and then act on it. I got a stack of big bills ready and cleaned up — suit, tie, the works. Drove a shiny car down a street in Beverly Hills or a place that sort of looked like Beverly Hills, a nice hotel all picked out ahead of time. I found a pretty woman who heard out my proposal, after the initial hassle and disbelief and a bunch of repetitions of you-got-to-be-kidding and show me the money. I added all the cool charm I could bring to it, just like Gere did. Money alone doesn't quite get it, you know. In a deal like this everybody's got to be comfortable. We're talkin' days not an hour or so.

The first surprise was her name. Hilda. Who could have foreseen that. Not Tempest. Not Boobs Star. Or Starr. None of that, just Hilda and no last name. There is never a last name. Except sometimes in the movies. Hilda. I couldn't get used to it. A wrinkle that made me wonder if I was doing it right. There was no well-turned out, sophisticated hotel manager. No one around to stick their nose up at her and later befriend her. No one treating me like I was a rich financial hotshot. No one who gave a rip — but, of course it wasn't a movie. I would probably have gone in this direction even if there had been no movie. I just wanted it to turn out like one.

In the hotel room I wanted to check out the bathroom. The tub. It wasn't right. It had no real ledge you could sit on and teasingly admire the woman in the water. I was scowling.

"What's wrong?," she said.

"The tub," I said, "it's too small."

"It seems like a normal tub," she said, looking at me strangely.

"It should be larger, big enough for both of us at once, me holding you in front of me, lots of suds and space and rich things laying around," gesturing with my hands.

"You're not going to get kinky are you?"

"No, of course not, just disappointed."

"Could we have a drink first and worry about this later," she asked.

"Sure," I said, coming to terms with it.

"What should we do afterwards," I asked tentatively.

"Afterwards?"

"Yeah, after...You know." She looked at me like a big sister looks at her dumb little brother.

"Maybe I'll just run away," she said, with a soft laugh and eyes that said, if I try it I expect you to stop me. She lifted her knees up so her chin could rest on them.

"No really," I insisted. "I promised you we would do a couple of things you never got to do. The stuff of your dreams. Remember?"

"Yeah, O.K.," she said, warming to it.

"Something I've wanted to do for a long time — I only got to do it once in my life."

"What?"

"Bowling. I want to go bowling."

"Bowling?"

"Yeah. Bowling. Whatsa matter with bowling? You got somethin' against bowling?"

"Bowling's fine." Crestfallen. "And after that?"

"Shopping!" Her hands clapped together. The eternal look of anticipation.

"Shopping?"

"Say Buster, it's your nickel, but it's the stuff of my dreams, right? Why don't we just do the stuff of your dreams, Geez!," hands on hips, disgusted, up and walking the length of the room and back again.

"Why didn't you just go to a brothel?"

"I was aiming a little higher."

"Well you haven't hit anything yet!"

"Hold it," my hand held up, a stop sign.

"Bowl and shop it is."

She jumped up in the air like a ten year old on a trampoline. "When do you want to start?"

"Whenever you say."

"Do you have an aunt Mabel?"

"What?"

"Do you have an aunt?"

"Honey, I got no relatives and none got me."

"One out of three."

"What?"

"Nothing. I can't explain it."

*

I supposed I had done it all wrong. Trying to invent myself from a film. Should have found a chick whose husband threw her out and asked her if she needed a place to crash for a couple of nights. No money. No dreams, no promises, no commitment. No questions, there might be answers. No resolution? Nothing is resolved. Nothing in life ever is.

*

Give it up. Get a dog.

*

Just a minute. The unmistakable woman walking up ahead. With the WALKMAN, music in her ear. Summer pony tail. Catch up. Walk along with her and…

BROCK'S ROAD

Why don't you come with us, a man called Brock said to me. We are standing at an airport bar and have only just met. He looks like Gable in his heyday with the insouciance to match. The girl behind the bar has told me I look like her grandpa fallen from a horse. Just teasing she insists. Not entirely I tell myself. I am flying north and Brock is driving south. He is waiting for a plane from Denver, carrying his sister and her girlfriend. Together with his chum, who is waiting outside, they will jump into a 4-wheel and race down highway 85 through Gila Bend and Ajo, crossing the border at Lukeville. Then dash across seventy miles or so of Mexican Sonora to Puerto Peñasco. Waiting for them is a trailer anchored in the sand of a trailer park and a long weekend on the coast. They will smoke pot all the way down and once there, swim until they nearly drown then get smashed. Drink so their eyes fall out. Sleep under the stars. Who could pass that up ain't livin' anyway.

I take his point. There is a depressing dignity in being a retired suit. This man is trying to save me from all the regal golf courses and walnut horseshoe piano bars where benevolent patriarchs hold your arm and say — did you hear the one about... He is going to cure me of an embarrassing disease. Besides, anything is better than the American daytime shit television yelling at us above the bar and which also follows me into every public place I go. It has been a long time since I have been down Brock's road. I want to go along. I want to go with them to where the mind shuts down and something new begins to appear. Put one foot in that part of Sonora and the other in the Gulf of California. I want to see what the sister and her friend look like. Rich girls from a big city disco or dirty-legged cowgirls, salty and warm, flecked with sand. Which one looks you straight in the eye and means what she says. Which one has the ankles to die for. Are these guys really good at this, or in the end they can't walk the walk. Saturday or Sunday or Monday, equilibrium lost — not from booze, but something somebody said in the midst of the sand flies, the scorpions — makes one of them a rooster hooded thereafter and all through the trip back.

He drains his drink and turns to me with a look that says — well? I tell him I can't. I wouldn't survive the trip. We wish each other luck. After he goes, I search the mirror on the wall behind the barmaid, looking for grandpa. I wish Brock had asked me thirty years ago.

TWENTIETH CENTURY
PLEASURES

I got on the little prop job and just sat there buckled in, listening to the motor rev and watching the blades spin outside the window. In a rare moment content to be just where I was. It didn't have the wonder of the first ride fifty years earlier but it suggested all the pleasure. How many more years would pass before piston engine planes with props, like the models I wound with my hand as a kid — even planes with wings — would be extinct. The young woman seated next to me had told me something of herself when she reached and uncrossed a cross-hatched seat belt so I could more easily take my place. In soft gray corduroy pants and a blue cloth coat, she was small town middle-America bound for big town middle-America. She didn't say so, but I knew she didn't want to go.

After we are up and out, the purring making the sleepy

sleepier, we start to bounce a little and then began to buck in earnest. She turned and threw herself into me, covering her mouth with one hand, the fingers of the other digging into my shoulder. I held her for a moment patting her back softly. We got rid of the big bumps quickly and she let go and kept her chin tucked tightly on clenched fists. When she held on to me I wanted to take it personally as if I mattered to her, not quite dim witted enough to believe she needed me; she didn't need me, she needed whoever was sitting next to her. Still, I didn't want her to let go and it was better than not being held at all. "Oh, I'm sorry," she said, as if that kind of intimacy with a stranger was a breach of some social contract. "Nothing to be sorry about," I replied. "Man's lucky to have a pretty girl next to him. Maybe the Holy Ghost put me on this bird so I could be of help" deliberately not looking at her, at once the sorry one for saying too much. As if invocation of a Holy Ghost were a breach of some social contract. She didn't seem to notice what I said. I sat there thinking about it anyway. At the start there were just a few people and a Holy Ghost could keep up. There are billions of people now. Far too many for a Holy Ghost to keep track of. Or it's somebody else's department anyway. I think it's a good thing I have not gone there with this out loud to her. I say nothing more. If she knew what I have learned about her from watching her, she might not like my taking something of her without her knowing it. She can rest easy. Whatever I know and don't know, she is safe.

Then again perhaps I can distract her. She is young enough for me to tell her something about the century she missed the better part of. A thing or two that's lost and won't come back. If she glazes over I will stop. I can tell her when it was legal to burn autumn leaves at city curbsides, the perfume sent up unlike any other. And how we took it for granted and now it has disappeared. What it was like to suck and then hold in your mouth a hint of pine in the ice shavings snatched off the back of the ice truck; trains that smelled like trains, pulled by steaming behemoths whose whistling sound was the voice of longing — wanting to get on so bad it was all I could think about. Town and country fireflies, the summers thick with them. It must have been right after that my long fall from paradise began. This time I hold my tongue. She is trying for a nap. I try too. Moving as close to her sleeping form as I can. She has no clue of the comfort she has given me. Déjà vu. I think I have known her always. The way the fabric holds her legs. The way she evades looking at me, until one day something I say clicks a ratchet in her heart and she decides it's time to sit on my lap, her hair whispering in my ear. She is not heavy, she is reassurance and with her rising up there comes an exaggerated loss. I imagine her connecting on to Kansas City, looking over her shoulder to see if I will follow. I do, but not right away. It takes me three days to find her again. Then we live together for three years straight. I shake my head at that and turn to her to see if she has heard my thoughts. She hasn't.

On the ground we goodbye abruptly, almost wooden. At

the luggage carousel the letdown of the real world overtakes me. As it was in the beginning, is now and ever shall be.

Time for coffee before standing in the taxi queue. Time for nearly anything — but the desire gone. I've been three men already — that's enough for one lifetime. All of them exist within, all but the last, alien. All sinners, the latest meek before the crook finger of God, is one of the children in the Book of Numbers sent out bewildered in the wilderness — though pray not forty years. Poor man, rich man — now beggarman begging hugs, begging to avoid surgery, Alzheimer's, nursing homes; still begging to differ with the twenty-first century which began before the calender said it would. Yet at the top of the hour and at the half, it is easy to enchant the body out of cold death for awhile. Just let music and memory touch a cheek and wait for my temperature to rise.

The ball I threw while playing in the park
Has not yet reached the ground —

Dylan Thomas

BIRTHDAY PRESENT

Can I help you?

That red rose over there.

Sure. One rose?

Please.

Special occasion?

Birthday.

Who's it for?

Girlfriend. Don't wrap it. She's waiting just up the road a way.

It's more of a surprise if I wrap it.

It's o.k. She's beyond surprise.

She's lucky to get a pretty rose.

I guess.

Hold it near the top, so you don't stick your fingers.

Yes Ma'am.

Here you are. I hope she likes it.

So do I.

SOLO DANCER

People said give it a year
We measure in these ways
A hundred yards
A thousand things
Decades
Millennia
Corners we turn
Easily
Old burdens swept aside
For a new dimension
On the smooth kitchen tile
He dances solo
Or leads the band
Miles Jamal Ellington
Ella's scat then Tormé
Whatever works
Has everything he needs
But a broomstick

ALL MY CHILDREN

They are fascinating. Even if sometimes you don't like them very much. You think they are too noisy. Intrusive. Brats. But oh baby, look at the way they look at you. A pair or pairs of eyes locked on to you, an explosion of curiosity. Some of them insisting on your undivided attention. Others clumping around a room deep in thought as though you did not exist. They are one or ten. Six or sixty. Children all of them. Some are all grown but the child in them persists, often dominating. They appear from nowhere for a minute, for an hour. Shrinking violets, magpies, St. Vitus's dancers, whippersnappers. To say nothing of the twigs, green shoots, beanpoles, barreltoes, two foot lumberjacks, pick one. Pick them all.

Children I never got to meet. Two Algerian boys and a girl in a pastel painting; Les Enfants du Pecheur. The fisherman's children have by now run away from childhood, perhaps from Algeria as well to some place where they thought real life would begin. But I have kept them in their frame. On the beach at Oran, the girl is still a girl holding a seashell and a basket of fruit. The usually drab, near invisible children of Lausanne-Prilly, extensions of a mother's coat sleeve, who placed flowers and notes written in sorrowful hands at the door of my apartment, the morning after JFK was killed. The boy who tends the lawns of the well-to-do, stops to retrieve a frog from a swimming pool. Puts the frog in his pocket and walks away, to cook or play with it nobody knows. His rake and shovel lay where he left them, old toys out of favor.

Johnny's puta in Buenos Aires. Eighteen tops. Always running off for licorice, then sticking out her black tongue at him when he complained about her black tongue. Johnny a large child himself at sixty, playing at belly bumping with anyone who will belly bump, saying you were a pissant and roaring like a bull of the pampas. The girl who threw Hammond's clothes out the fourth floor hotel window when he wouldn't pay her. The girl gone. Hammond naked on the phone trying to get someone to go and at least bring up his pants. The little chicklet waitress in a tavern, after telling me they have no gin brings a beer with an olive in it. The urge to safekeep the wretched and the disreputable. Sometimes you see more of them when you think of them later. Details in shadow when you were looking right at them.

My child toddling through a store, who pulled a pacifier

from another child's mouth and put it in her own. My child who did not. Children in a children's hospital. The one I am holding, clutching tighter, is not a patient. The one we are looking at drives a fire truck, looks up at my prize, his I.V. set up trailing him, guided by a nurse. Children in a neighborhood. The silent and the sullen on their bikes demonically pedaling away from a speaking part, fleeing ties that bind. Others of another camp, quick to smile and wave, waiting before they move on for a small verbal jab. These are the tree climbers, lemonade sellers, songsingers, apothecaries to the heart. My child who held her nose while sitting a horse. My child who did not.

August morning on the south side of the house. Me in my bed just awake, in a new emptiness. Hearing "GAK!" and then a giggle from the one year old in the kitchen. I rise and go to her as if my salvation is in her language.

It is or will be May, June, July. I have coffee, cold water, hot sun, the whole of an afternoon. And all my children.

> *de Fog come on itty bitty kitty*
> *footies. He sit down on Chicago*
> *— and whammo he gone.*

Carl Sandburg
(version for his grandchildren)

LADY, LADY

Memory. The spinster aunt who adored you, came to call you "Suzy Red Pants." Why the Suzy, who knew. The red pants were your panties. She would grin, blushing as though spilling a great secret she had shared with you. Lord knows you didn't parade in them. You were then for her and mother a proxy daughter. Not recent history. Most young women had scarlet dresses, not scarlet lingerie. Were you Miss or Mrs? A distinction lost on me. A photo of you at twenty, holding an open umbrella in front of you, just so, giving the impression you are wearing nothing. It was not taken for me. It might as well have been. About then I came into your life and your umbrella disappeared. A shield you could put down, like those weapons of the mind, earrings, unneeded or fumbled away in the dark, time-proofed theaters I hid you in. For a time I became the usurper of your affection. Trouble was, trouble keeping my hands off you. Stuck them in with yours in your winter muff, my pockets useless.

Reflection, said Rita Dove, is such a bloodless light. Push on. The end of a wedding reception in the here and now. I swim the room looking for and not finding you. The groom holds the bride at the front door. They take a deep breath and plunge down the steps into darkness, as members of their honor guard on either side drum them with flower petals. It is a wonder they do not fall. Did we do this? Soon there will be no one who remembers.

Fittings. The ring. It fit. All that oohing and aahing. Big Jim calling you "Mrs. Gotrocks." Where did I get the money? All I know is I didn't borrow or steal it. The dresses. They fit too. The saleswoman amused as I with my hands construct a size. About like this here, like that there. Almost flat where the pleats begin to fall. Practice. Practice. We have the feeling we're O.K. Safe. No. Not safe. If safe is inseparable. Whatever stirs us, we can say it or leave it unsaid. Inhabit each other naturally. In war, the door half open to peace. Rarely a mature tongue-and-groove trunk lid fit. Transient husband. Flirt and run. Honeymoons like rabbits, multiplying. Hunkering down for the coming empty nest.

Crossings. The days pile on and we begin that slow roll off the earth. You in your private sorrow. Me in my public profanity. An odd pair sometimes at odds over what comes to nothing. I wanted to give you something more than a drink of water. I wanted to tell you something, anything, but all my masks deserted me. I was a ghostly nurse. Lady, Lady. I tried not to fear my life or yours, fear the end of things. We knew what the two of us couldn't say. Some of us learn hard lessons. You were the abundance the world gives and often I looked the other way, as if the world gave more.

This sounds too much like regret. There is always that. We were good and lucky too. Tell it. Tell instead about our season. How we held each other in forms of grace and consolation. About dancing on air. And those bright, vanishing years we ran through.

> *The man is staring across the threshold*
> *And cannot recognize his home*
> *Every line of her had gone*
> *To the bottom of his soul*

Boris Pasternak

THE ASH AND THE LOCUST

They are at Mendota — M'dota, meeting of the waters —
the junction of the Mississippi and Minnesota rivers.
When General Sibley saw it, he said it was an absolute
wild save where the flag floated at Fort Snelling. It was
handed down that Colonel Snelling said it was so empty
that the trees had only each other to talk to. That's
probably where it all started.

The cemetery is small, old and still. It seems always in a
provincial autumn. The stones a mixture of sarcophagal
sculpture, obelisk, rolltop, thick arrowhead and more
recently, polished granite. They are beneath one of these,
above the rivers, between an ash and a locust tree. Squared
off and trenched deep into their surroundings, done with
the shovelman, out of harm's way. She had worked her
angel stint on earth. He was by turns a thistle and a feather
in the wind.

From one generation to the next, most belief excludes the
spectral. Spirits of the dead do not mix with the living. And
sycamores do not speak in sycamore. That's the
conventional wisdom. But then you know about the limits
of conventional wisdom. Everybody lives around here
seems to know about… Deloite. It was old Deloite made
the bell ring in the church across the road, the church
locked and no one beneath the bellrope. A bell so heavy it
could not have been rung by a gust or by itself. Why him?
In life he whacked his own tube chimes with leather-
headed mallets. O'Ryan, was it, on clear nights, not even a
scent of dew, makes, when he wants, clear water run over
gravel, then overlays it with hailstone, powder blue. Except
O'Ryan's been under a rock since eighteen sixty-five.
Thomas, believing he is kin to Dylan, stands at the front, as
though he were a film noir border guard, in the night a
glowing bush challenging anyone who enters. If you look
for him in daylight he is where everyone thinks he is; to
some he is the bland, woody, rotund perennial on the right.
And so it goes.

Is she the ash with the fruit, sheltering. Or the locust with
the graceful flowers, leaves blue-green like her eyes. She is
the one, someone says. She is the other, says another. Who
knew enough of them and who has heard them whisper in
the night. The yardman says it is too soon. No one knows
in drifts of sleep they come upon each other, no need of
language, reaching out like water falling in a dream.

We live by gesture. The utterly intimate glimpse a grace unbestowed. Still, there were enough riches in her smile to make a world. He knew that. And before the key turned and the bolt ran on him he knew he must follow her here. In the beginning she had made him live and in the end he would die of her.

> *...For a thing once set in motion*
> *has no ending in this world*
> *until the last witness has passed.*

Cormac McCarthy